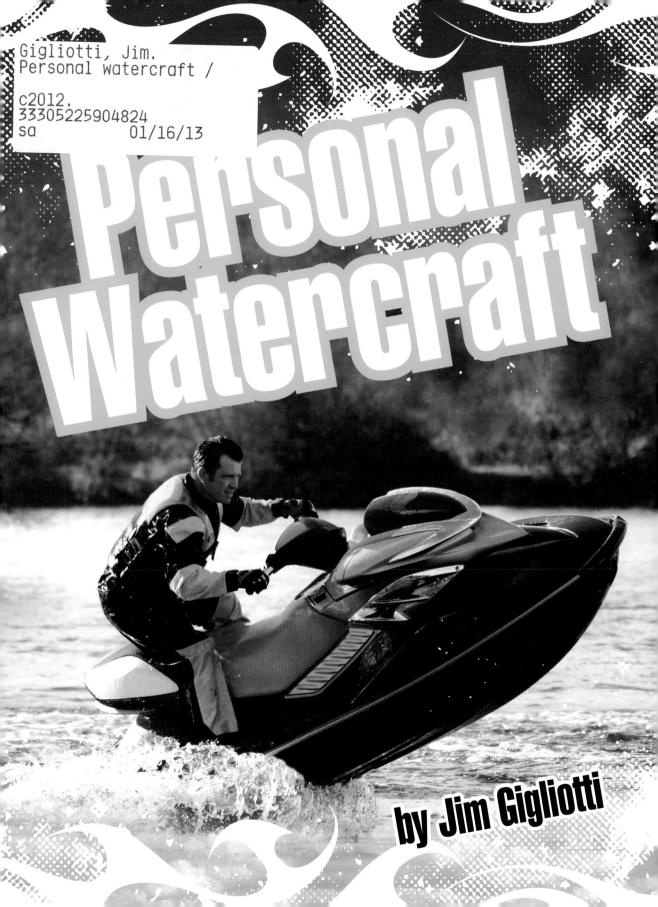

Personal Watercraft

by Jim Gigliotti

Published by The Child's World®
1980 Lookout Drive
Mankato, MN 56003-1705
800-599-READ
www.childsworld.com

The Child's World®: Mary Berendes, Publishing Director
Shoreline Publishing Group, LLC: James Buckley Jr.,
   Production Director
The Design Lab: Design and production

ISBN 9781609731809
LCCN 2011940083

Photo credits: Cover: Photos.com.
Interior: AP/Wide World: 7; dreamstime.com: Gustavo
Fernades 11, Anatoliy Samara 20; iStock: 19, 24,
28; Young Huynh/PWCOffshore.com: 4; Courtesy
Kawasaki: 12; Photos.com: 8, 15, 16, 23, 27.

Printed in the United States of America

Table of Contents

Top racer Kim Bushong roars into action.

CHAPTER ONE

And They're Off!

More than 40 riders are lined up near the famous *Queen Mary* ocean liner in Long Beach, California.

The orange flag goes up. The air is filled with the throaty roar of each of their engines revving at once.

The green flag goes down. With a mighty rumble and a burst of speed, they bolt from the starting line!

Sound like a motocross race? Or maybe the famous Long Beach Grand Prix Indy Car race? Well, on some days it could be either one . . . but on this day in the summer of 2010, it's the annual LB2CAT personal watercraft long-distance race. "LB" is for "Long Beach." The number "2" stands in for the word "to." "CAT" is short for "Santa Catalina Island," more commonly called Catalina. The event is 58 miles of exciting, high-speed, offshore racing. These athletes have taken the sport of riding personal watercraft (or PWC, for short) to a new extreme: They're riding in the open ocean.

The start line for the riders is actually in the water. They race 29 miles (47 km) across the sea—with **swells** this year reaching as high as 5 feet beyond the break wall—to a "turn boat" off the coast of Catalina. (Catalina is a small island southwest of Los Angeles.) Then the racers turn around and head back to where they started. They can travel at speeds of almost 70 miles per hour (113 kph), and complete the trip in less than an hour. In 2010, Kim Bushong won the race on a Kawasaki Ultra 250X Jet Ski. Two-time defending champion Craig Warner, also riding a Kawasaki, had the lead early in the race but had to drop out with mechanical difficulties.

PWCs take part in high-speed racing action around the world; this racer is near Cyprus, an island in the Mediterranean Sea.

A powerful PWC turns water-lovers into speed demons!

The LB2CAT is part of the American Power Boat Association's (APBA) Offshore national championships. It's one of three legs of offshore racing's "Triple Crown," along with other races off the California coast. The Triple Crown began in 2009. Offshore racing is a pretty new way to race.

While the racers, most PWC riders are just regular folks looking for fun on the water. They ride PWCs on rivers, lakes, and near sunny beaches. Since these craft were invented, millions of people have turned the surface of the water into a race track!

The original PWC was called the Sea-Doo. It was invented by an American named Clayton Jacobson II in the 1960s. Jacobson was a banker in Arizona who liked to ride motocross in his spare time. He wanted to bring something like motocross to the water. So he quit his job as a banker and developed a **prototype** of the PWC. The Bombardier Corporation, which already made the Ski-Doo snowmobile, began selling the Sea-Doo PWC in 1968.

PWCs rapidly grew in popularity—but not just for racing. In fact, while some experienced riders like the ones in the LB2CAT and other events love to compete in races and **freestyle** competitions, most of the estimated 30 million or so PWC riders are in it just to enjoy some fun on the water.

Freestyle riders take their PWCs to extremes!

The Jet Ski is the most well-known type of PWC.

You'll often hear PWC riding referred to as "jet skiing." The two terms usually mean the same thing, but Jet Ski is actually a brand name. That means it is a specific type of personal watercraft manufactured by Kawasaki. Jet Skis became so popular that they soon became **synonymous** with PWC riding. (It's kind of like when all facial tissues are called Kleenex or all adhesive writing pads are called Post-it Notes.) In addition to the Jet Ski, other popular PWCs include the Waverunner by Yamaha, and the Sea-Doo by Bombardier.

Whatever you call these watery speed machines, anyone who rides one will tell you: All they care about is the fun!

CHAPTER TWO

Getting Started

Before we look at how to ride a PWC, let's look at how they work. Motorboats have a metal propeller that spins very fast under the boat. The propeller makes the boat move forward. Unlike motorboats, a PWC has an "impeller" on the inside. This does the same work as a boat's propeller, but inside the machine instead of outside. The curved blades of the impeller suck water into the PWC from a hole in the bottom of the vehicle. It propels the water out the back. That water is **expelled** with such force that the pressure causes the PWC to move forward. Look closely at a photo of a Jet Ski or other PWC, and you'll see a stream of water shooting out!

PWCs can help a group of friends have a great time on the water.

Many beach resorts have PWCs for guests to use.
Warm water is a great place to ride a PWC.

Before you pick out a PWC that's right for you, you need to be safe in the water. No matter how good you get at riding a PWC, you will end up in the water some of the time!

The most important step to water safety is learning how to swim. Take swim lessons from a qualified instructor, and learn to be comfortable in the water. Once you've become a good swimmer, learn your local rules. Since PWCs are really a kind of boat, all states have boating rules and laws. In some states, you'll need to be a certain age before you can get on a PWC. The web site of the American Boating Association (americanboating.org) is a good place to find out more.

Regardless of the rules, kids should never ride a PWC without a grownup. The adult should start the PWC and wear the **lanyard** with the automatic shut-off pin. (If a rider falls into the water, the pin comes out of the vehicle. This immediately shuts the machine off to keep the PWC from going away on its own.) Always wear a life jacket and a wetsuit, safety glasses, footwear, and gloves.

When you get on the water, use common sense. The U.S. Coast Guard Auxiliary offers plenty of safety tips. Among them: practice safe boating; never spray other vessels or jump in the wakes of other boats; maintain a safe speed; and know your limits, as well as your PWC's limits.

RIding with an adult is the best way for kids to get the fun of zooming along on a PWC.

Push the red button to start the PWC. Twist the handle on the right to make the machine go faster.

After you've had the proper training and obtained the proper safety equipment, it's important to pick out the PWC that's right for you. The original PWCs were single-person models on which the rider stood. The more popular models now are sit-down versions. Most sit one or two people (though a few larger ones can sit three or even four people).

Driving a PWC is actually fairly easy. Most have electric push-button starters. The **throttle** is on a hand grip. Twist it backward to make the machine go forward. The handlebars work much like a bicycle or scooter. Then to make the machine stop, just let go of the throttle.

It does take practice, but once you've got the hang of it, you'll be zipping across the water with the wind in your face!

CHAPTER THREE

Relax . . . or Race!

These days, everybody seems to enjoy getting on a PWC.

It was the middle of summer in 2010, and almost time for training camp. But before heading off to practice football, Arizona Cardinals star wide receiver Larry Fitzgerald Tweeted a photo of him and his son riding their Sea-Doo on Minnesota's Lake Bryant.

On a Christmas vacation in 2010, actress Cameron Diaz and New York Yankees infielder Alex Rodriguez rode their Waverunners off the coast of Mexico. Photos popped up in gossip magazines and newspapers around the world.

PWCs are often seen in the movies, on television shows, and in commercials, too. But you don't have to be a professional athlete or a celebrity to enjoy riding a PWC. It's a great way to relax and enjoy some vacation time on the water.

When Alex Rodriguez is not catching ground balls,
he caught some rays during a PWC ride.

A PWC race on a lake always starts with the roar of a pack of engines!

For the PWC rider who wants to more than just relax, there are more and more ways to race!

The International Jet Sports Boating Association (IJSBA) holds amateur and pro events around the world. Each fall, the IJSBA holds the annual World Finals in Lake Havasu, Arizona. In 2010, riders from almost 40 counties competed in 44 race divisions at the World Finals.

IJSBA racers compete in many different formats. Closed-course races are like motocross races. Riders navigate a course, often about a half-mile long, a specified number of times. In drag races, riders compete in brief spurts over a shorter distance, usually one-eighth of one mile. Endurance races are offshore, long-distance events. Freestyle events test a rider's ability to perform creative **maneuvers** in a two-minute time limit. Slalom events are just like ski slaloms. Riders zigzag their way left and right through a specified series of markers as fast as they can and with as few errors as possible.

PWCs are easy to handle. They're powerful enough to move quickly, and small enough to maneuver in spaces that other boats can't. So that makes PWCs a valuable resource for rescue and law-enforcement personnel, too.

Hurricane Ike slammed down near Galveston, Texas, in the summer of 2008. Rescue workers searched the damage while riding PWCs. On lakes and rivers, officials use PWCs to enforce the law. Lifeguards can hop on a PWC to quickly reach an accident victim out in the water and bring him or her to the shore. Stretchers attached to the PWC let them carry victims safely.

Lifeguards drive PWCs with rescue sleds attached to the back. Swimmers in trouble can climb on and get a ride back to shore.

Up and over! Expert freestyle riders can do flips such as this one.

PWCs are used in racing and for rescues. For most PWC enthusiasts, though, the fun is simply in gliding along the surface and feeling the warmth of the sun, the cool of the breeze, and the cool spray of the water. More experienced riders can carve a turn that would make a surfer proud . . . or do a barrel roll that would be the envy of any wakeboarder! But those kinds of moves, as well as riding in the ocean like the racers in Chapter 1, are not for beginners. They're strictly for experts. But if you keep riding and learn . . . someday you'll be an expert, too.

Glossary

expelled—forced out

freestyle—a competition in which participants can use any moves they want to impress judges

lanyard—a cord or line fastened to the rider

maneuvers—movements or tactics

prototype—a model of a product that will be made in the future

swells—a series of waves

synonymous—a different word that has the same meaning

throttle—a switch that sends power to an engine

Find Out More

BOOKS

Jet Ski (Built for Speed)
By Luke Thompson (2000, Children's Press)
This book offers a brief history of personal watercraft, plus valuable tips for PWC safety.

Riding Waverunners (Action Sports)
By Kelli Hicks (2009, Rourke Publishing)
What is a waverunner? How does it work? This book answers those questions . . . and more!

WEB SITES

For links to learn more about extreme sports: **childsworld.com/links**

Note to Parents, Teachers, and Librarians: We routinely verify our Web links to make sure they are safe and active sites. So encourage your readers to check them out!

Index

About the Author

Jim Gigliotti is a former editor at the National Football League. He has written more than 50 books about sports for youngsters and adults.